Bluegrass and Old-Time Fiddle Tunes for Harmonica

by Glenn Weiser

 To access audio, visit:
www.HalLeonard.com/MyLibrary
Enter Code
7928-1024-6836-1859

Design & Typography by Roy "Rick" Dains
FalconMarketingMedia@gmail.com

ISBN 978-1-57424-345-1

Foreword
by Charlie McCoy

I just had a look at a new book by Glenn Weiser of 67 traditional fiddle tunes for harmonica. The harmonica tablature is straight ahead and easy to follow. Most of these fiddle tunes come from Celtic music, which I am really fond of. Thanks, Glenn, for making these tunes known to harmonica players, and for showing them the way to play them.

Table of Contents

Technical Notes, Part I - Single Note Tunes

1. Music Notation. All tunes here are notated in their original fiddle keys with guitar chords provided so that this book may double as a tunebook for players of other instruments. You have to know how to read rhythms in combination with the tablature to play the tunes, but fortunately typical fiddle rhythms are easy to read. My book Irish and American Fiddle Tunes for Harmonica explains how to read common fiddle rhythms, and I will also be posting videos of myself playing the tunes on my website, www.celticguitarmusic.com. MIDI files can be found on the Hal Leonard website.

2. Harmonica Tablature. Circled hole numbers under the notation indicate draw reeds, while uncircled numbers indicate blow reeds. A single "V" under a hole number indicates a half-step note bend, while a double "V" indicates a whole-step bend.

3. Pucker technique. I play single note tunes with pucker technique. For this, you need to form your lips into a vertical oval which can then play the harmonica one note at a time. There are four main elements of getting a single note on the harmonica: place the harmonica on the inside of your lips, keep your lips relaxed, lower your jaw, and pinch in with the corners of your mouth. Done correctly, this will produce a single note. Once you can do this, there are three main techniques for getting around the harmonica: slurs, the "ta" articulation, and the breath stop.

• **Slurs.** When going between two or more adjacent holes of the same breath direction, simply continue the breath you began the first note with. This will make for a smoother melodic line.

• **The "ta" articulation.** When repeating a note or a chord, touch the tip of your tongue to the roof of your mouth above your front teeth as if whispering the syllable "ta." This will make the notes more distinct. The "ta" articulation can also be used in eighth note rhythms when going between two notes of the same breath direction which are separated by one or more holes to avoid sounding them.

• **The breath stop.** When going between two notes of the same breath direction which are separated by one or more holes in slower rhythms (quarter notes or greater), simply cut your breath short to avoid sounding the intervening holes.

4. Chords. Guitar chords have been provided for the tunes. Because the old-time backup guitarists of the 1920s and 30s generally avoided minor chords and the modal VII, some modern pickers follow suit in order to recreate the sound of the early string bands. But coming from a Celtic music background, those chords in old-time music sound natural to my ear, and so I have used them sparingly here. Feel free to play whichever chords you prefer.

Introduction

This is a collection of 67 bluegrass and old-time fiddle tunes arranged for 10-hole diatonic harmonicas, complete with music notation in the original fiddle keys, harmonica tablature, and guitar chords. Here you will find many of the best known traditional tunes in these genres, among them "Blackberry Blossom," "Bill Cheatham," "John Brown's Dream," Breaking Up Christmas," and more.

The story of country music begins with the string bands of the 1920s, when most of these tunes were first recorded, and the harmonica was there from the start. On December 12th, 1923, the Okeh label issued "Rain Crow Bill," "The Old Time Fox Chase," and "Lost Train Blues" by Henry Whitter, a Virginia mill hand. Later in the 1920s, Fate Norris waxed a version of "Turkey in the Straw" with the Skillet Lickers, and Dr. Humphrey Bate and His Possum Hunters played on WWSM in Nashville and recorded "The Eighth of January" and other fiddle tunes. The warbling harmonica of Garley Foster took over the usual lead role of the fiddle altogether in the Carolina Tar Heels, and there were many others. In the bluegrass world, Bill Monroe's first lineup of the Bluegrass Boys included Thurman "Curley" Bradshaw, who played rack-mounted harmonica along with his guitar (unfortunately, Bradshaw doesn't seem to have ever recorded the harp with Monroe due to the WWII recording ban). In the 1960s Wayne Raney accompanied the Stanley Brothers, and Charlie McCoy recorded "Liberty" with Flatt and Scruggs. And of course, McCoy's version of "The Orange Blossom Special" is the most famous harmonica fiddle tune of them all.

To contribute to this tradition, here is my second volume of fiddle tunes for harmonica. The first, Irish and American Fiddle Tunes for Harmonica, was published in 1987 by Centerstream and has over 100 reels, jigs, and hornpipes. A few of the tunes from that book that were originally arranged for the 12-hole diatonic have been rearranged here for Paddy Richter tuning, an alteration devised by Brendan Power in 1993 that changes the 3-draw reed from the fifth step of the major scale to the sixth (the fifth step is also found on the 2-draw). This makes the tunes that I first wrote for the 12-hole easier to play. There are over a dozen tunes in this book tabbed for Paddy Richter harmonicas in G, A, C, and D, and several tunes are tabbed for both standard and Paddy Ritchter. Paddy-tuned harmonicas are made by Seydel and sold through Musician's Friend. In addition, I have arranged 10 tunes for tongue-blocking style harmonica, showing how some of the old-timers such as Earnest "Pop" Stoneman played chords to accompany his single note melodies.

You will be able to hear recordings of the tunes from this book on my website, www.celticguitarmusic.com, on YouTube, and on the Hal Leonard website as well.

Lastly, I also offer private lessons on Skype for anyone wishing to study these tunes or other styles of music with me on harmonica, guitar, banjo, ukulele, and mandolin. See my website for details.

Enjoy the music.

Glenn Weiser
Southwick, MA

Abe's Retreat

Also known as the "The Battle of Bull Run," this haunting Dorian mode tune
comes from West Virginia, and is based on the banjo playing of Craig Duncan.

Paddy Richter G- Harmonica

Traditional, Arr. G. Weiser

Copyright 2016 G. Weiser

Avalon Quickstep

This tune was recorded by Narmour & Smith in 1930 and has a 10-bar B part; the version here comes from the playing of the Arm and Hammer String Band. Avalon MS, after which the tune is named, is also famous as the home town of country bluesman Mississippi John Hurt.

D-Harmonica

Traditional, Arr. G. Weiser

The Big Scioty

The Scioto River, which this tune is titled after, flows through Ohio and empties into the Ohio
River. This version was transcribed from the playing of bluegrass mandolinist Adam Steffey.

G-Harmonica

Traditional, Arr. G. Weiser

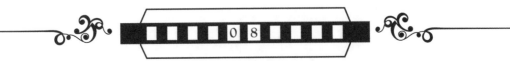

Bill Cheatham

First recoreded by Eck Robertson in 1922, this is one of the most popular
old-time tunes in bluegrass music. This version is based on printed sources.

Paddy Richter A-Harmonica

Traditional, Arr. G. Weiser

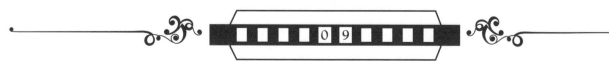

Billy in the Lowground

This a famous American tune that has several possible Celtic ancestors (see the
website The Fiddler's Companion for the details on this one and all others).
The version here is based on that of Doc Watson, except that in his version the
second note of the fourth measure of the B part is a B, and I've substituted a C.

C-Harmonica

Traditional, Arr. G. Weiser

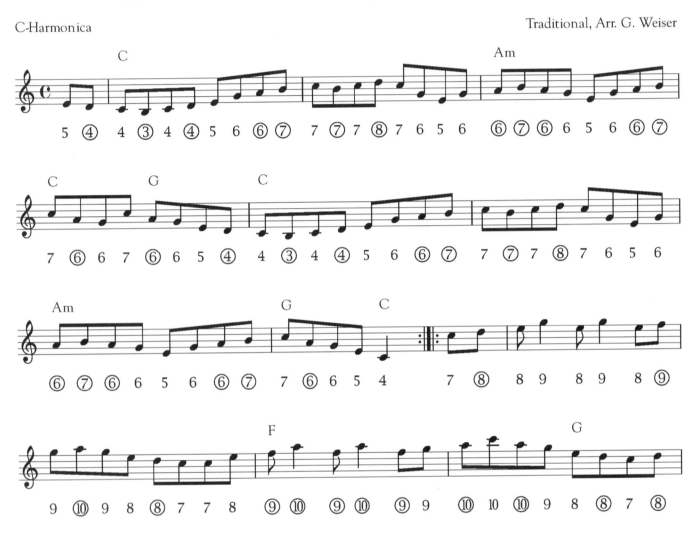

Blackberry Blossom

This bluegrass standard was first recorded by Fiddlin' Arthur Smith in 1929 and is also
popular with Irish musicians. This version comes from bluegrass mandolinist Jack Tottle.

Paddy Richter G-Harmonica

Traditional, Arr. G. Weiser

Boil Them Cabbage Down

This famous hoedown was recorded by the Dixie Crackers in 1929.
I adapted it for the harmonica from the fiddling of Tommy Jackson.

Traditional, Arr. G. Weiser

A-Harmonica

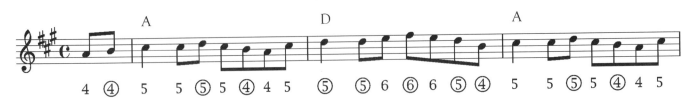

4 ④ 5 5 ⑤ 5 ④ 4 5 ⑤ ⑤ 6 ⑥ 6 ⑤ ④ 5 5 ⑤ 5 ④ 4 5

④ ④ 5 ④ 4 ④ 5 ④ 5 ⑤ 5 ④ 4 5 ⑤ 5 ⑤ 6 ⑥ ⑦ 7 ⑤

5 ④ 4 5 ④ 4 ③ ④ 4 4 ④ 4 5 ⑤ 6 ⑥ 6 ⑤ 5 ⑤

6 ⑥ 6 5 ⑤ 6 6 ⑥ 6 ⑤ 5 ④ 5 ④ 5 ⑤ 6 6 ⑥ 6 5 4 5

⑤ 5 ⑤ 6 ⑥ ⑦ 7 ⑥ 6 ⑤ 5 4 ④ 4 ③ ④ 4 4 ④ 4

Booth Shot Lincoln

This old-time tune commemorates the April 14th, 1865, assassination of President
Abraham Lincoln by the actor John Wilkes Booth at Ford's Theater, Washington,
D.C., during a performance of a play. This was recorded by Bascomb Lamar Lunsford
in 1949; the version here was transcribed from the fiddling of Emily Phillips.

Paddy Richter A-Harmonica

Traditional, Arr. G. Weiser

Boston Boy

Bill Monroe learned this old reel from his uncle, fiddler Pen Vandiver, and popularized
it with bluegrass players. Transcribed from the fiddling of Kenny Baker with Monroe.

C-Harmonica

Traditional, Arr. G. Weiser

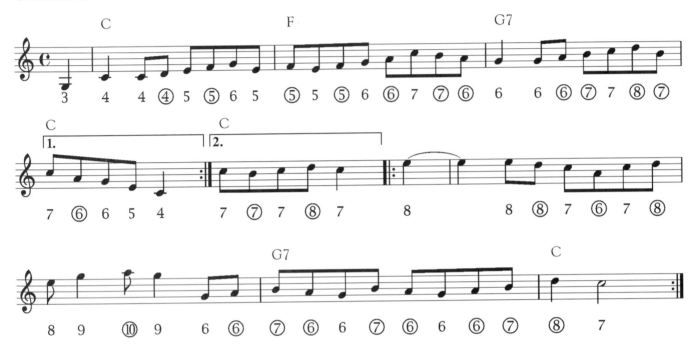

Cluck Old Hen

This is a Dorian mode version of this famous tune, recorded in 1927 by The Hill Billies.
Jerry Garcia picks it breifly on *Shady Grove*, his 1996 album with David Grisman.

G-Harmonica, top row tab, Paddy Richter, botton row.

Traditional, Arr. G. Weiser

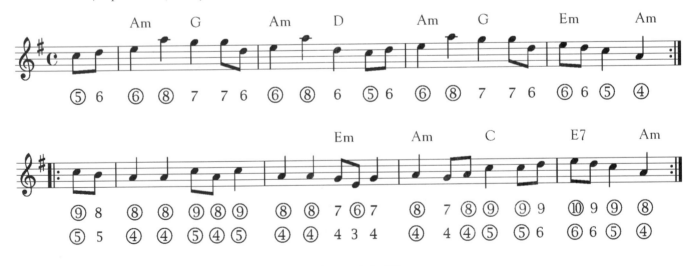

Breaking Up Christmas

This North Carolina breakdown is a must-know tune for old-time musicians.
In 1752, England switched from the Julian calendar to the Gregorian, which meant
that the 12 days of Christamas, which had been celebrated beginning on the Gregorian
equivalent of January 6, then began on December 25. Hence the tune's title.
The version here is based on the variants of Tommy Jarrell and Bruce Molsky.

Paddy Richter A-Harmonica

Traditional, Arr. G. Weiser

Campbell's Farewell to Redgap

This Mixolydian mode tune is desecended from the Scottish pipe march, "Campbell's Farewell to Redcastle." This version is based on the fiddling of Wayne Cantwell.

D-Harmonica

Traditional, Arr. G. Weiser

The Cherokee Shuffle

This tune developed out an older breakdown called "Lonesome Indian" and is popular with bluegrass players. In the B part, note the releasing grace note half-step bends on the first two notes of the fourth and eighth measures. For this, begin the note bent, and then let it quickly rise. This version is my own composite.

Paddy Richter A-Harmonica

Traditional, Arr. G. Weiser

Cold Frosty Morning

Alan Jabbor collected this Dorian mode tune from Virginia fiddler Henry Reed in 1966. This tune and others later on can played on either a standard 10-hole or a Paddy Richter -tuned harp. Follow the top or bottom row of the tab of the A part dependending on which tuning you are using. The tab for the B part is the same on either model.

G-Harmonica, top row tab, Paddy Richter, bottom row.

Traditional, Arr. G. Weiser

Cotton-Eyed Joe

Widely known in the South, it is thought this breakdown comes from Texas. This was recorded in 1928 by the Skillet Lickers; the version here is based on the fiddling of Tex Logan with Bill Monroe.

A-Harmonica, top row tab, Paddy Richter, bottom row.

Traditional, Arr. G. Weiser

Cumberland Gap

In 1775 Daniel Boone and his company of axmen blazed the Wilderness Road through the Cumberland Gap, a mountain pass near the Kentucky-Tennessee-Virginia tri-state border. Over the next few decades, an estimated 250,000 settlers would pass through the gap to settle the lands west of the Blue Ridge and Great Smoky mountains. This was recorded in 1928 by The Skillet Lickers; the version here is based on the fiddling of Jane Rothfield with Brendan Power.

D-Harmonica, top row tab, Paddy Richter, bottom row.

Traditional, Arr. G. Weiser

Fine Times at Our House

This Mixolydian mode breakdown comes from West Virginia fiddler Edwin Hammons, and is a "crooked" tune with its odd measure of 5/4. This should be played with a swing eighth feel. Transcribed from the playing of Stephanie Coleman. Paddy Richter tab is provided for the last measure, which uses a note bend on the standard 10- hole.

D-Harmonica, Paddy Richter, bottom row.

Traditional, Arr. G. Weiser

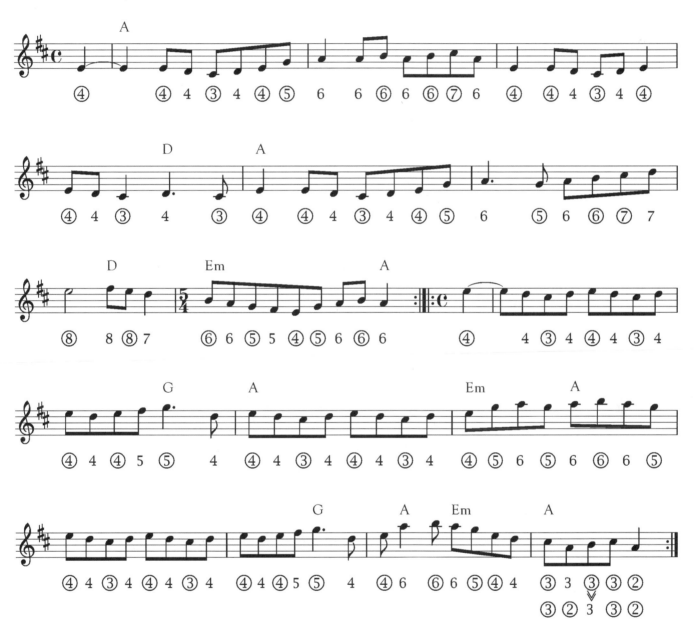

Flop-Eared Mule

I learned this tune from Woody Vermiere, a West Coast fiddler who I knew in high school in New Jersey. It was recored by Charlie Poole and the Highlanders in 1929; this my own version.

Traditional, Arr. G. Weiser

D-Harmonica

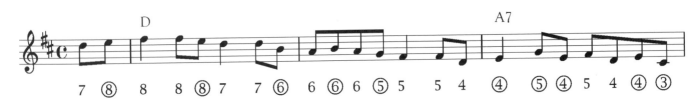

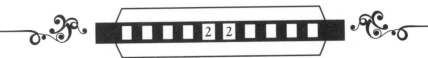

The Flowers of Edinburgh

This tune is a Scottish reel that I found the fiddler Fletcher Bright playing at a jam at his house up on Lookout Mountain in Tennessee. The title may refer to a neighborhood of the city known as The Flowers, or the belles of the town. Canadian fiddler Don Messer recorded the tune in 1947; the version here is based on the banjo playing of Ken Perlman.

Paddy Richter G-Harmonica

Traditional, Arr. G. Weiser

The Flying Cloud Cotillion

A cotillion is a type of fiddle tune that has the A and B parts in different keys.
Therefore you need two harmonicas, one for each part, to play this. The tune was
named after the famous clipper ship, and was recorded by The North Carolina
Ramblers in 1926. The version here is based on the banjo playing of Bob Carlin.

G and D Harmonicas   Traditional, Arr. G. Weiser

Forked Deer

This popular breakdown could be a descendent of the Scottish tune "Rachel Rae,"
which it resembles. The Forked Deer River flows through western Tennessee, and is
the likely source of the title. The tune, first published in 1839, is also known as "Bragg's
Retreat," which probably refers to the 1863 Tullahoma Campaign of the Civil War.
It was recorded by Charlie Bowman in 1929; the version here is my own composite.

D-Harmonica

Traditional, Arr. G. Weiser

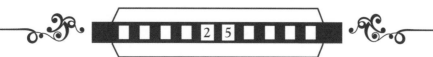

Fortune

Popular in the Galax, VA area, this tune was collected by Miles Krassen.
The version here is based on the fiddling of Otis Burris and Eddie Bond.

Paddy Richter D-Harmonica

Traditional, Arr. G. Weiser

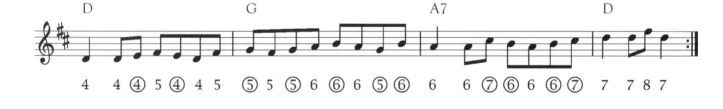

Goodbye, Liza Jane

I first heard this tune in Tennessee, where I was teaching at the
Folk School of Chattanooga. This was recorded by Fiddling John
Carson in 1926; the version here is my own composite.

G-Harmonica, top row tab, Paddy Richter, bottom row.

Traditional, Arr. G. Weiser

The Hangman's Reel

It is thought that this polular breakdown evolved out of the Quebecois tune
"The Hanged Man's Reel." Transcribed from the fiddling of Darol Anger.

Paddy Richter A-Harmonica

Traditional, Arr. G. Weiser

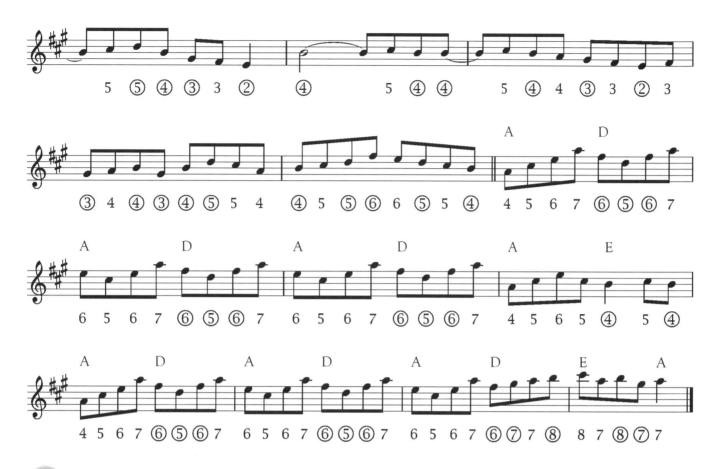

The Fairy Dance (Old Molly Hare)

Rarely in old-time music can we trace a centuries-old tune back to a known composer.
"Old Molly Hare" is the descendant of "The Fairy Dance," written by the Scottish
fiddler Nathaniel Gow for the Fife Hunt Ball of 1802. This is the original.

D-Harmonica, top row tab, Paddy Richter, bottom row.

Neil Gow, Arr. G. Weiser

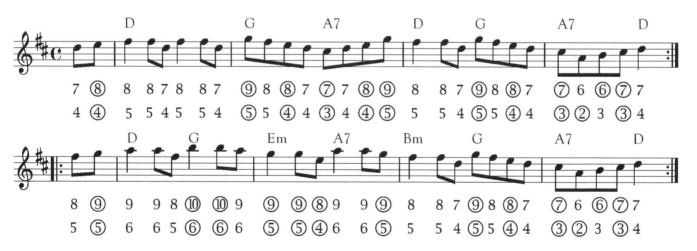

Hop High Ladies

This is the descendant of the Scottish tune "Miss McLeod's Reel." It was
recorded in 1926 by the North Carolina Ramblers under the title "Mountain
Reel." The version here is my own composite of a few different settings.

G-Harmonica

Traditional, Arr. G. Weiser

Jimmy in the Swamp

This tune originated in eastern Kentucky and later spread to the Midwest.
You can hear Norman and Nancy Blake play this on the album *Warehouse
Tracks*. This version is based on the 1951 recording by Bob Walters as printed
in the indespensible *The Milliner-Koken Collection of American Fiddle Tunes*.

Paddy Richter G-Harmonica

Traditional, Arr. G. Weiser

John Brown's Dream

If there were such a thing as the Old-Time Top 40, this one would be a chart
topper. The musical interest of tunes like this often lies more in what a good
fiddler can do with them rather than the plainspoken melodies themselves.
Play this one with a strong backbeat - accents on the second and fourth beats
of the measures. This was recored by Da Costa Woltz's Southern Broadcasters
in 1927; the version here is based on those of Tommy Jarrell and Bruce Molsky.

A-Harmonica

Traditional, Arr. G. Weiser

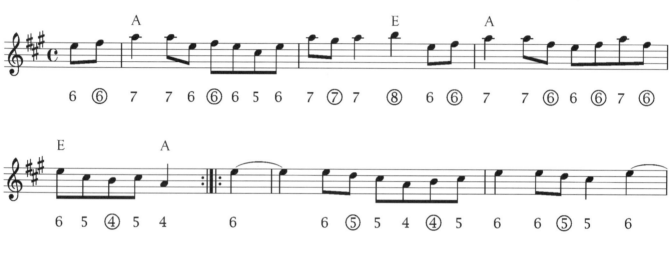

Johnny Don't Get Drunk

This breakdown is said to come from Missouri and is based on the fiddling of
Emily Phillips. It was recorded in 1970 by John Ashby the Free State Ramblers.

D-Harmonica

Traditional, Arr. G. Weiser

June Apple

A June apple is an early ripening variety that is smaller and more tart than those which mature later in the growing season. This tune comes from Virginia and is in the Mixolydian mode. It was collected by Miles Krassen from Ben Jarrell and Uncle Charlie Higgins.

D-Harmonica

Traditional, Arr. G. Weiser

Katy Hill

This breakdown is known throughout the South and Midwest, and became a showpiece for fiddlers on the Grand Ole Opry. This was recoreded in 1928 by Lowell Stokes; the version here is from abcnotation.com, a fabulous online repository of sheet music for hundreds of thousands of traditional tunes.

Paddy Richter G-Harmonica

Traditional, Arr. G. Weiser

Leather Breeches

This is considered the descendant of the Scottish tune "Lord MacDonald's Reel." "Leather breeches"
is also a nickname for snap beans. This was recored by Uncle Am Stuart in 1924, the version
here was transcribed from the playing of Emily Phillips, an Arkansas state fiddle champion.

G-Harmonica

Traditional, Arr. G. Weiser

Magpie

This bouncy tune comes from North Carolina, and has an A part which closely resembles "Evan's Hornpipe." This was collected by Alan Jabbour in 1966 from the fiddle-banjo duo Harlan Coble and Lonnie Corsbie; the version here is my own composite from YouTube and printed sources.

G - Harmonica

Traditional, arr. G. Weiser

2016 G. Weiser

Mississippi Sawyer

This old-time reel is descended from the Irish march "The Downfall of Paris," one of the many tunes the Irish named after Napoleon in a vain attempt to woo Bonaparte into attacking England and liberating the Emerald Isle. 'Mississippi sawyer' was a term for a tree which had fallen into the big river but was still connected by its roots to the bank, thus endangering passing steamboats. The Skillet Lickers recorded this one in 1929. Note that in the fourth bar of the B part you have to bend the 3-draw reed down a whole step. Paddy Richter tab has also been provided for that measure and elsewhere.

D-Harmonica, Paddy Richter, bottom row.

Traditional, Arr. G. Weiser

Old Dan Tucker

Rev. Dan Tucker was a Revolutionary War veteran who took a land grant and settled in Elbery County in Georgia, where he operated Tucker's Ferry near his home. The song was popularized by the Virginia Minstrels in 1843 and recorded by The Skillet Lickers in 1928. Transcribed from the fiddling of Tim O'Brien.

D-Harmonica, top row tab, Paddy Richter, bottom row.

Traditional, Arr. G. Weiser

The Old Gray Cat

This is an Irish reel that I found some pickers playing at the Snow Hill Bluegrass
Jamboree near Chattanooga. I never met a fiddle tune in E minor I didn't like.

D-Harmonica

Traditional, Arr. G. Weiser

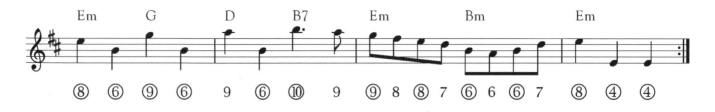

Old Mother Flanigan

This old-time tune is descended from the Irish reel "The Greenfields of America."

A-Harmonica, top row tab, Paddy Richter, bottom row

Traditional, Arr. G. Weiser

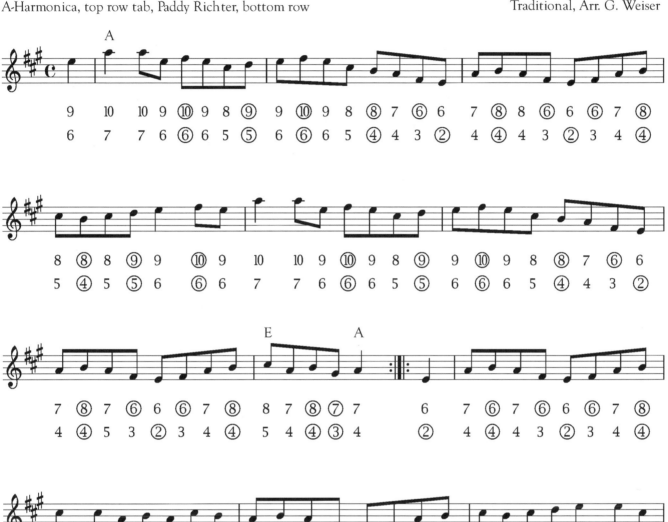

Pig Ankle Rag

This is an old fiddle rag that was recorded in 1928 by harmonica player Noah Lewis with Gus Cannon's Jug Stompers. The version here is based on that of the Highwoods String Band.

D-Harmonica

Traditional, Arr. G. Weiser

Ragtime Annie

First recorded by Eck Robertson in 1923, this is my own composite version for harmonica.

D-Harmonica

Traditional, Arr. G. Weiser

Red Wing

In 1907 Kerry Kills took the opening of Robert Schmann's "The Happy Farmer," and wrote
a Tin Pan Alley song about an Indian maiden pining for her brave that became a fiddle
chestnut. This version is my embellishment of the tune. To hear a similar exmaple of how
to fancy up a song in old-time style, listen to the Skillett Lickers' rendition of "Dixie."

Paddy Richter G-Harmonica

Kerry Mills, Arr. G. Weiser

Richmond Cotillion

This is another cotillion, meaning that the A and B parts are in different keys, so you'll need
two harmonicas to play this. DaCosta Woltz's Southern Broadcasters recorded this one in 1927.

D and A Harmonicas

Traditional, Arr. G. Weiser

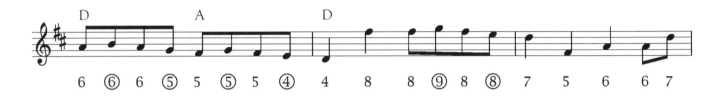

Sail Away Ladies

This was recorded by Uncle Bunt Stevens in 1926. Transcribed from the fiddling of Kenny Baker. Baker alternates the C part with the A part, so the order of the parts is A-B-C-B. In the penultimate measure of the C part, he throws in a blue note, a Bb, that I have rendered here as a B natural.

Paddy Richter G-Harmonica

Traditional, Arr. G. Weiser

Sally Ann

This Appalchian old-time tune was recorded by The Hill Billies in 1925 and is
a favorite among bluegrass bands. Transcribed from the fiddling of Ian Walsh.

A-Harmonica, top row tab, Paddy Richter, bottom row.

Traditional, Arr. G. Weiser

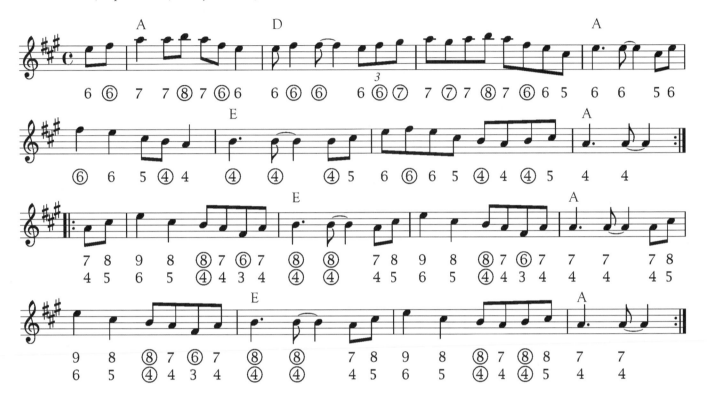

Sally Goodin

This tune is played throughout the South. During the Civil War, a company of musical Conferate soldiers
camped by a boarding house on the Big Sandy River in Kentucky run by one Sally Goodin and wrote and
named the tune for her. This was recorded by Eck Robertson in 1922; the version here is my own composite.

G-Harmonica

Traditional, Arr. G. Weiser

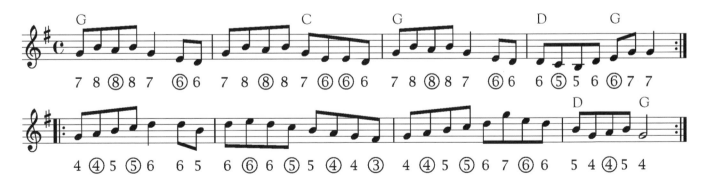

Salt Creek

This was recored as "Salt River" by the Kessinger Brothers in 1929; Bill Monroe
retitled it in his 1963 recording with banjoist Bill Keith. On the third note
in the last measure of the B part you have to bend the 3-draw reed down
by a whole step. Paddy Richter tab has also been provided for that measure.

D-Harmonica, Paddy Richter, bottom row tab.

Traditional, Arr. G. Weiser

Copyright 2016 G. Weiser

Shenandoah Falls

This is an old-time tune of obscure origin popularized by Vermont fiddler Pete Sutherland.
Note the ragtime type syncopations. This one should be played with a swing eighth feel.
Paddy Richter tab has been provided for the B part, only two notes in the A part need it.

A-Harmonica, top row tab, Paddy Richter, bottom row.   Traditional, Arr. G. Weiser

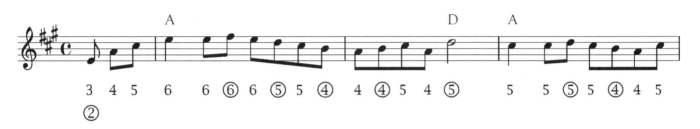

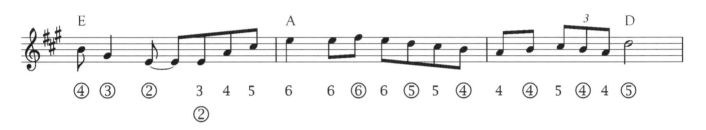

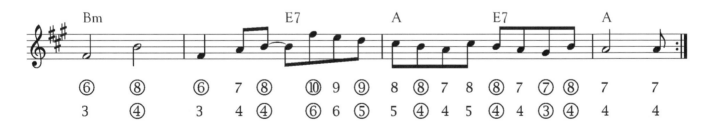

Copyright 2016 G. Weiser

Shove That Pig's Foot a Little Farther in the Fire

This charming old-time tune was originally recorded by North Carolina fiddler Martin Marcus.
The version here is based on a duet version played by Jay Ungar and Bruce Molsky.

G-Harmonica

Traditional, Arr. G. Weiser

The Smoke Above the Clouds

This tune is a musical memento from Chattanooga, Tennessee, where I lived from 2012-2014.
The title refers to the Battle of Lookout Mountain, which was fought on Novemeber 24th,
1963. On that day the Union forces under Gen. Joeseph Hooker drove the Confererates led by
Gen. Carter Stevenson off the peak overlooking Chattanooga. Although low-hanging clouds hid
the fighting from the view of the city's residents, they could see the smoke from the guns rising
over the mist. Hence the engagement's nickname, 'The Battle Above the Clouds.' This was recorded
by Jess Young in 1925 and transcribed from the fiddling of Jim Cauthen with the band Flying Jenny.

G-Harmonica

Traditional, Arr. G. Weiser

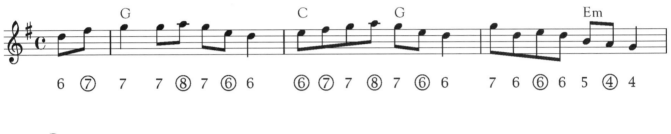

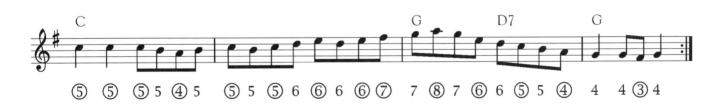

Soldier's Joy

This is a different setting of "Soldier's Joy" than the one in my earlier collection,
Irish and Amercian Fiddle Tunes for Harmonica. The variant here is close to the version
recorded by The Skillet Lickers in 1929. The tune dates back to the 18th Century and
was called "The King's Head." During the Civil War, a cocktail of whiskey, beer, and morphine
known as 'soldier's joy' was given to wounded troops, and the tune itself was played after the
war to welcome Confederate soldiers home. It is among the most famous of all fiddle tunes.

D-Harmonica

Traditional, Arr. G. Weiser

The Squirrel Hunters

In the summer of 1862, 15,000 Ohio men were mustered to defend the city of Cincinatti from a feared attack by Confederate forces in Kentucky under General Kirby Smith. These Union troops were known as 'The Squirrel Hunters'. The assault, though, never came and the Squirrel Hunters were disbanded. This Mixolydian mode tune was transcribed from the playing of mandolinist Sharon Gilchrist.

D-Harmonica

Traditional, Arr. G. Weiser

Stoney Point

I learned this Revolutionary War tune from the LP *Ninth Annual Banjo Contest: Craftsbury Common, VT,* on which it is played by Bob Poor. The title commemorates the 1779 victory of the American forces under Gen. Anthony Wayne over the British led by Sir Henry Clinton at Stoney Point, NY.

G-Harmonica

Traditional, Arr. G. Weiser

The Temperance Reel

From *Cole's 1000 Fiddle Tunes*, where is appears as "The Teetotaler's Reel." It was first recorded by Joeseph Samuels in 1919. In some versions of the tune, the first note of the B part, third measure, is a B (5-blow) instead of an A (4-draw, marked with an asterisk). The B can be substituted for the A if you find the fast jumps between the 6-blow notes too tricky.

Paddy Richter G-Harmonica

Traditional, Arr. G. Weiser

Tennessee Wagoner

Found everywhere form Arkansas to upstate New York, this tune had a fill-in-the-blank title
like "Buffalo Gals" and hence turns up with various state names. Note that in the fourth bar
of the B part you have to bend the 3-draw reed down a whole step. This was the first tune fiddled
by Uncle Jimmy Thompson over Nashville's WSM Barn Dance, the show that later became
the Grand Ole Opry, on November 18, 1925. Transcribed from the fiddling of April Verch.

C-Harmonica, Paddy Richter, bottom row.

Traditional, Arr. G. Weiser

Too Young to Marry

This is an old-time tune found in North Carolina and Virginia. I learned
this variant from the traditional musicians around Albany, NY in the
1980s. It was recorded by the North Carolina Ramlers in 1926.

D-Harmonica

Traditional, Arr. G. Weiser

Waynesboro

This old-time tune is descended from the Irish reel "Over the Moor to Maggie." It was recorded by Doc Roberts in 1927; the variant here is based on the version played by fiddler Alan Jabbour. Waynesboro is a town in the Shenandoah Valley of Virginia.

A-Harmonica, top row tab, Paddy Richter, bottom row.

Traditional, Arr. G. Weiser

Whiskey Before Breakfast

This tune originated in Canada's Maritime provinces, where it was known as "Spirits of the Morning," and is now widely played in the USA. The version here is my own composite.

Paddy Richter D-Harmonica

Traditional, Arr. G. Weiser

D · · · · · · · · · · · · G · D

② 4 ④ 5 ⑤ 6 6 5 6 ⑥ 6 ⑤ 5 ④ 4 5 ⑤ ⑥ ⑤ 5 6 5

A · · · · · · · · · · · · D

④ 5 ④ 4 ③ 3 ② 4 ④ 5 ⑤ 6 6 5 6 ⑥ 6 ⑤ 5 ④ 4 5

G · · · D · · · A · · · D

⑤ ⑥ ⑤ 4 5 4 ④ 4 ④ 5 4 6 ⑤ 5 6 ⑥ ⑦ 7 7 ⑧

· · · · · · · · Em · · · · · · A7

8 ⑧ 7 ⑦ ⑥ 6 ⑧ ⑧ 7 ⑧ ⑧ 8 ⑨ 8 ⑧ 7 ⑦ 6 ⑥ ⑦

D · A · G · D · G · D · A · D

7 8 7 ⑦ ⑧ ⑦ ⑥ 6 ⑥ ⑦ 7 6 5 4 ⑤ ⑥ ⑤ 5 6 5 ④ 4 ④ 5 4

The Yellow Rose of Texas

This is an example of a fiddle tune that grew out of a song, in this case one about
the slave girl who according to legend amorously detained Santa Anna in his tent
on the day of the Battle of San Jacinto in 1836, thus enabling the Texan forces under
Sam Houston to have the element of surprise and rout the Mexican army. Recorded
in 1927 by Da Costa Woltz's Southern Broadcasters, this is my own composite.

D-Harmonica

Traditional, Arr. G. Weiser

Technical Notes, Part 2 - Tongue Blocking

The 10 tunes in this section are intended to be played with tongue blocking technique. In tongue blocking, you play a single note melody with the right side of the mouth while your tongue moves to the left and lifts and presses back down onto the three holes to the left of the melody note, playing a chord line below the tune (Pucker players can ignore the tongue-block line and just play the single note melody). Here are some instructions and exercises to get you started with tongue blocking.

1. Basic Tongue Blocking. To get a single note with tongue blocking, first cover four holes with your mouth. Then shift you tongue to the left in such a way that allows you to play a single hole on the right side of the harmonica as shown below. Make sure that you're not hearing any low notes when the tongue is down.

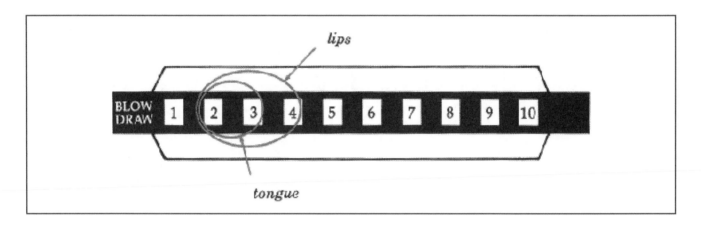

2. When you can do this, try playing some easy single note melodies like "Oh! Susanna" or "Skip to My Lou" with your tongue down on the three lower holes. Then practice lifting the tongue, blowing and drawing on all four holes, and then replacing the tongue so that you are playing the same single hole again.

3. Tongue blocking is written here in a two-staff format. The single note melody is on the top stave, and the line with the chords produced by the tongue, which are also called slaps, is on the lower stave. The tongue chords are represented by notes with circled or uncircled 'x's to represent draw chords or blow chords respectively. All tongue chords, whether notated as quarter notes or eighth notes, are to be played staccato, that is, very clipped.

Exercise 1 shows you two kinds of chords played by the tongue: the basic slap, which is played with the melody note, and the lift, which is a slap that is played after the melody note. The melody, the major scale, is in half notes with quarter note chords (although in practice the slaps sound more like eighth notes followed by eighth rests). Exercise 2 consists of an ascending major scale with slaps. Exercise 3 is a descending major scale with lifts.

Technical Notes, Part 2 - Tongue Blocking

Ex. 1 - Half-note scale, quarter note tongue slaps.

Ex. 2 - Quarter note scale with onbeat slaps.　　　Ex. 3 - Quarter note scale with offbeat slaps.

Exercise 4 shows you some different melodic rhythms with quarter and eighth note slaps.

4a uses the Nashville shuffle, which is a quarter-eighth-eighth fiddle bowing pattern. Slap quickly on "1," then slap again on "2." On "2+," lift your tongue up, and slap on "3," etc. It's a slap-slap-

lift sequence on harp. **4b** shows two different slap patterns for the dotted quarter-eighth rhythm figure. The first is slap-slap-lift and the second is slap-slap-rest. **4c** shows slaps on all the onbeats in a running eighth note scale. You can find most of the chord patterns in the songs in these exercises. Practice them slowly at first.

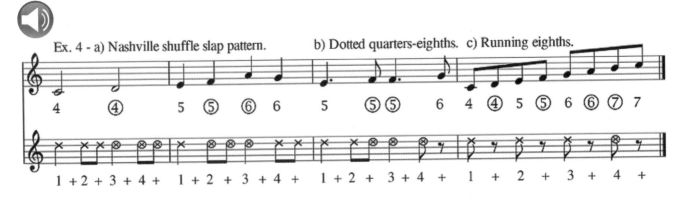

Ex. 4 - a) Nashville shuffle slap pattern.　　b) Dotted quarters-eighths. c) Running eighths.

Angeline The Baker

This fiddle tune grew out of the chorus of the Stephen Foster song,
"Angelina Baker." It was recorded by Uncle Eck Dunford in 1928.

D-Harmonica

Traditional, Arr. G. Weiser

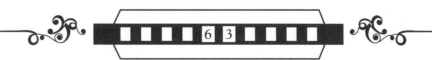

Bonaparte Crossing the Rhine

This robust march appears to be related to earlier
Irish tunes, and is often played at old-time sessions.

D-Harmonica

Traditional, Arr. G. Weiser

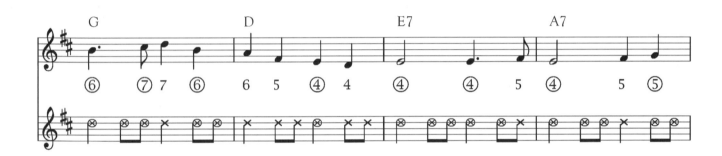

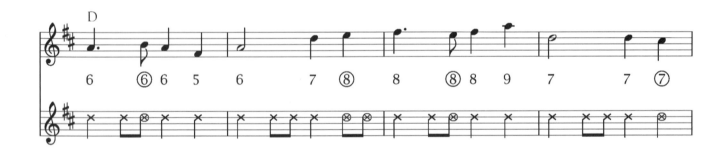

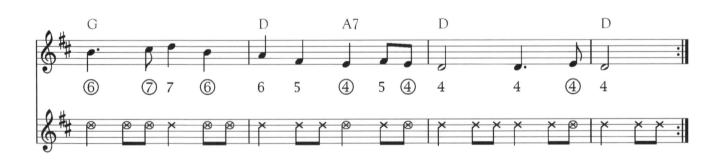

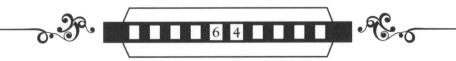

Bonaparte Crossing the Rhine

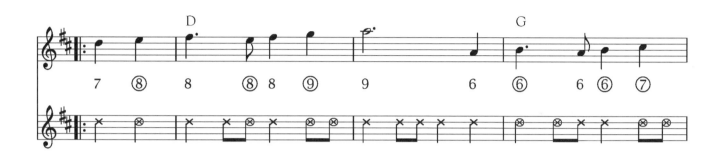

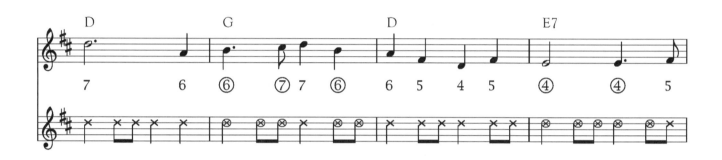

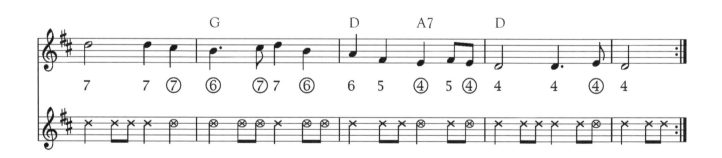

Bonaparte's Retreat

I larned this version of the famous old-time tune during an offstage jam with
fiddler Alan Jabbour and banjoist Ken Perlman when we were performing
at the 2006 Old Songs Festival. It was recorded by A. A. Gray in 1924.
Napoleon set out for Russia in 1812 with 400,000 men and returned with 10,000.

D-Harmonica

Traditional, Arr. G. Weiser

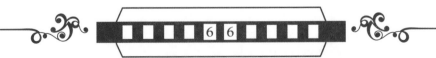

Coleman's March

In 1847, the wife of Kentucky shoemaker and fiddler Joe Coleman went missing. Coleman was convicted of her murder and sentenced to hang. On his way to the gallows, he rode in a cart sitting on his coffin and played this slow 4/4 version of a 6/8 song, "The Irish Jaunting Car." As fate would have it, the hangman botched the execution and Coleman survived, unconscious. His family spirited him away, after which he recovered fully and left the state, never to be heard from again.

D-Harmonica

Traditional, Arr. G Weiser

Darling Nellie Gray

Benjamin Hanby, a college student in Ohio, wrote this song in 1856 to
publicize the plight of an escaped slave from Kentucky whose sweetheart
had been sold to a man in Georgia. It became very poular in the North
and helped fuel the growing abolitionist sentiment of the public there.
This was recorded by George Wade and His Corn Huskers in 1931.

G-Harmonica

Benjamin Hanby, Arr. G. Weiser

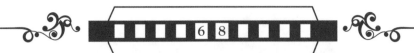

Darling Nellie Gray

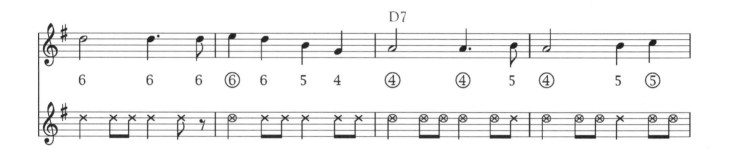

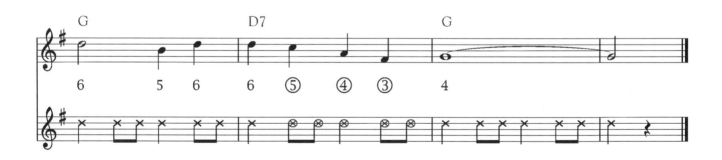

Oh! Dem Golden Slippers

This was written by James A. Bland in 1879 as a minstrel show parody of the spiritual "Golden Slippers," which the Fisk Jubilee Singers had made famous. The spoof was performed in blackface in its time before becoming a standard bluegrass instrumental. It is also the theme song of the annual Philadelpia Mummers' Parade. This was recorded by Vernon Dalhart and Carson Robison in 1928.

D-Haronica

James A. Bland, Arr. G. Weiser

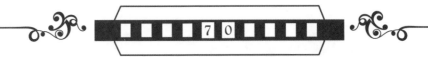

Oh! Dem Golden Slippers

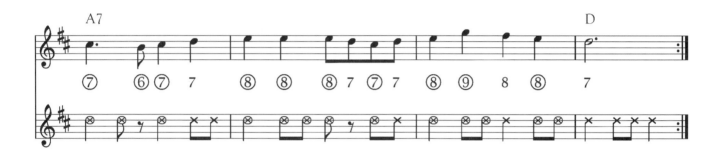

Songwriter, Carson J. Robison (left)
and singer, Vernon Dalhart (right).

My Grandfather's Clock

Before this 1876 song was published, what we now know as grandfathers' clocks were called tall clocks. The enormous popularity of this song, though, changed the name of that common household item forever. Work based his lyrics on the true story of a hotel owner in England whose tall clock stopped ticking at the moment of his death. This was recorded by the Carolina Buddies in 1935.

G-Harmonica

Henry Clay Work, Arr. G. Weiser

My Grandfather's Clock

Home Sweet Home

Composed by Henry Bishop in 1823, this became a bluegrass
standard when Earl Scruggs released his banjo version in 1961.
Da Costa Woltz's Southern Broadcasters recorded it in 1927.

G-Harmonica

Henry Bishop, Arr. G. Weiser

The Seneca Square Dance

Also known as "Waiting for the Federals," this tune comes from
the Midwest. It was recorded by Ozark fiddler Sam Long in 1926.

G-Harmonica

Traditional, Arr. G. Weiser.

Copyright 2016 G. Weiser

Listen to the Mockingbird

This 1855 popular ballad was a favorite song of Abraham Lincoln, who, according to an unproven claim by his biographer Carl Sandburg, was also a harmonica player. It has become a fiddle contest standard, to which competitors add birdcall imitations and other effects. I switch to pucker position when playing the groups of four eighth notes. This was recorded by Arthur Smith in 1935.

D-Harmonica

Alice Hawthorne, Arr. G. Weiser

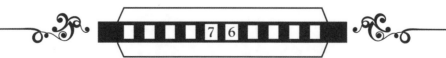

Listen to the Mockingbird

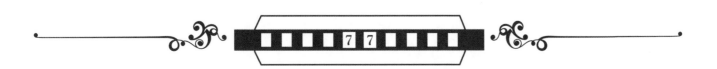

Acknowledgements

I would like to thank the many people who, directly or indirectly, had a role in the birth of this book.

First, my publisher, Ron Middlebrook of Centerstream Publications, for bringing out the book. I'd also like to thank Charlie McCoy for writing out the foreword. Gratitude is also due to my wife Patti, a former graphic designer, for her help with typesetting the text.

I prepared the tunes in this book with MuseScore, a free open-source, Linux-based music notation program. I would like to thank Marc Sabatella and the other resident experts of the MuseScore online forum who were always available whenever I had questions about the software. I would also like to thank Winslow Xerxa for supplying me with the Richter harmonica tab font used here.

If you put ten fiddlers in a room and had them take turns playing the same tune, you would probably hear ten different versions of it (and here I'll relay some advice from fiddler Alan Kaufman -when you're at an old-time jam, sit out the tune once or twice and just listen to it so you can adapt your version to the one the group is playing). Some settings of a given breakdown will always be more interesting than others, and therefore if no satisfactory printed source is available, arriving at the most melodious variant can take some doing. For this, sometimes I created composite versions, a method also used by the folk song collector Alan Lomax and more recently by Miles Krassen in his 1973 book Appalachian Fiddle, but often I found fine versions on YouTube. So I'd like to thank the many fiddlers, mandolinists, and banjo players both famous and obscure whose online video performances provided me with tunes that I either transcribed note-for-note or tinkered with slightly: Darol Anger, Justin Belew, Wayne Cantwell, Jim Cauthen, Stephanie Coleman, Craig Duncan, Sharon Gilchrist, Alan Jabbour, Stephen Lind, Jake Loew, Bruce Molsky, Tim O'Brien, Emily Phillips, Jane Rothfield, Adam Steffey, Jay Ungar, April Verch, and Ian Walsh.

Lastly, I'd like to tip my hat to the harmonica players who are out there performing fiddle music and raising awareness that so many of the old breakdowns, reels and jigs can be played on this instrument: Donald Black, James Conway, Cara Cooke, Paul Davies, Jim Etkin, Tony Eyers, Mark Graham, Trip Henderson, David Naiditch, Brendan Power, David Rice, Seth Shumate, and Mike Stevens.

- G.W.

"Well, there it goes again . . . Every night when we bed down, that confounded harmonica starts in."